CAPTIVE of
PITTSFORD RIDGE

JANICE OVECKA

THE NEW ENGLAND PRESS
Shelburne, Vermont

For David

Manufactured in the United States of America
First Edition
Cover illustration by Elayne Sears
Design by Andrea Gray

For additional copies of this book or for a catalog
of our other titles, please write:

The New England Press
P.O. Box 575
Shelburne, VT 05482

Ovecka, Janice, 1956-
    Captive of Pittsford Ridge / Janice Ovecka
        p.   cm.
    Summary: In 1777 when he rescues a wounded Hessian drummer, young Josiah Freeman is drawn into the fighting at the Battle of Hubbardton near his family's farm in Vermont.
    ISBN 1-881535-11-8 : $10.95
    1. Vermont—History—Revolution, 1775–1783—Juvenile fiction.
[1. Vermont—History—Revolution, 1775–1783—Fiction. 2. Frontier and pioneer life—Vermont—Fiction.] I. Title.
PZ7.0944Cap   1994
[Fic]—dc20   94-24533
                                                   CIP
                                                   AC

—CONTENTS—

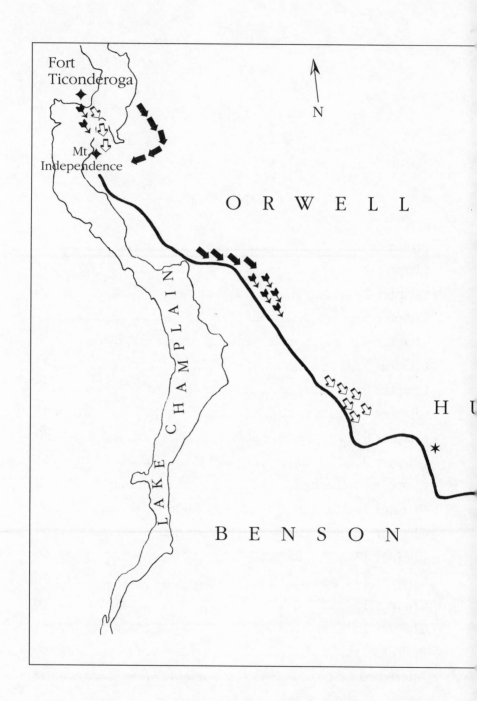

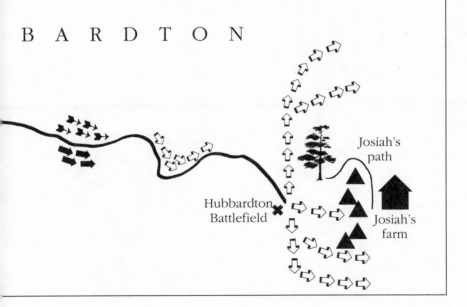

KEY

⇨ Americans
➤➤ British
➡ Germans
▲ Pittsford Ridge
✦ fort
✳ Captain Johnson stops to rest
✖ Hubbardton Battlefield

PITTSFORD

BARDTON

Josiah's
path

Hubbardton
Battlefield

Josiah's
farm

— *P*ROLOGUE —

East Hubbardton, Vermont
June 1994

The school bus rolled to a stop, and Andrea Freeman stood up in her seat to look out at the broad meadows and green mountains beyond. It was the last field trip of the year, and Miss Cline had brought them to the Hubbardton Battlefield. Some of the children had grumbled about seeing a dumb old battlefield, but Andrea was excited.

"I had an ancestor who fought in the Hubbardton battle," she yelled to her friend Julie as the children lined up to get off the bus.

"Yeah, right," said Julie, punching her way into line.

Andrea pushed in behind her. "No, really," she said. "A great-great-something. He had a farm on the other side of those mountains. My grandma told me."

Julie's reply was lost in the din. Andrea followed her off the bus and looked around eagerly. There was a white

1

visitors' center. To one side stood some picnic benches and a tall white monument enclosed in a black metal fence. The rest of the class went inside the enclosure, and Andrea, who lingered outside, saw Miss Cline pointing to the shaft and talking. Just as Andrea got to the fence, Miss Cline directed the children into the visitors' center. Andrea stayed behind to look at the monument.

She squinted up at the marble shaft. "Hmmm . . . 'Colonel Seth Warner, Colonel Ebenezer Francis, Colonel Nathan Hale.' No Freeman there. Oh well, maybe he was just a plain soldier." She ran to join her class inside the building.

A guide was telling the group all about the American Revolutionary War and how the Americans fought the British here at Hubbardton as they fled south from Fort Ticonderoga. Andrea listened for a moment, then wandered off. She looked at the charts and maps on the wall. There were many pictures of soldiers—even a little drummer boy in a colorful uniform.

Over in a corner was a diorama in a glass case. Andrea was drawn to it and stood staring at the tiny figures.

It was a battle scene. In front were the Americans, behind a stone wall on top of a hill. Up the hill came soldiers in red coats. They were the British, and up the hill they came, advancing steadily. . . .

—CHAPTER 1—

Mount Independence, Vermont
July 6, 1777 4:00 a.m.

Chaos reigned as men milled about on the hillside fort of Mount Independence, Vermont. On the other side of Lake Champlain, the British had occupied Fort Ticonderoga only an hour earlier. The retreating American troops had damaged the connecting bridge across the lake, but scouts reported that the British were about to cross the lake to attack from the west. The lake was narrow enough that it would not be long before British boats landed, and the bridge would not take long for the redcoats to repair. Their German allies were already on the lake's eastern shore and were bearing down on the mount from the north. There was little time left to evacuate Mount Independence and move on.

Flames shot into the night as a building caught fire. Captain William Johnson of the Green Mountain Boys swore softly under his breath—so much for a quiet retreat. The newer recruits were panicking and rushing about, some stealing the liquor stores and drinking until they could hardly stagger. The officers in charge had their work cut out for them, reforming the lines to move out down the military road to the south.

Captain Johnson's men stood in a tight group away from the general confusion. They were alert and watchful, and as seasoned soldiers, they remained calm as the first of the quickly formed regiments moved off. Johnson motioned to his men.

"Form a line here," he said in a low voice. "Colonel Francis has ordered us to be the rear guard. We have to hold off the enemy coming from the north. The scouts say the Germans are getting close. Captain Freeman's unit is covering the retreat from the shore. When they get to the road, we'll follow. Remember, no unnecessary shooting." His white teeth flashed against his dark beard.

The men moved to the shelter of some felled trees and watched the dark woods. Behind them, the glow of the burning buildings lit up the forms of the marching men. The retreat was going more quickly now, and the rest of the main army was preparing to leave. The humid July night pressed down on Captain Johnson's men as they waited, watching and listening. Mosquitoes whined in their ears, but soon they heard another sound—the distant beating of drums.

"That's them," said Captain Johnson. "The Germans always have their drummer boys with them." He glanced behind at the road south. "Just a few more minutes, and we'll be on our way."

The beating grew nearer, and the men tensed, muskets held ready. Captain Johnson's heart pounded, matching the beat of the drums. A shot rang out.

"Easy now," whispered Captain Johnson. "They're almost in range, then we'll give it to them."

Out of the corner of his eye he saw Captain Freeman's unit running to the road.

"Fire!" he yelled, and the men rose and fired, the sound tearing through the heavy air. They crouched again as their volley was answered, musket balls singing past them.

"To the road!" shouted Captain Johnson, and his men ran to catch up with the others. He turned for one last look, but not even the lightening sky brightened the shadows of the trees where the Germans gathered. Still, they were there, no doubt, marching onward and beating their drums as they came.

—— CHAPTER 2 ——

Pittsford, Vermont
July 6, 1777 Daybreak

Josiah Freeman knelt by the side of the brook and splashed water on his face. It was cool and refreshing as he combed his wet fingers through his hair. He eyed the brook longingly—how nice it would be to go wading! But now was not the time—there were chores to do.

He picked up two buckets and dipped them into the brook. His father had partly dammed the brook years before and created a deep pool where water could be drawn easily. Last spring he had added an improvement— a series of hollow logs that formed a pipeline down to a trough outside the cabin. But Mother used that water only for washing and watering the animals. She preferred the freshly drawn water for cooking.

Josiah quickly dipped his kerchief into the water and tied it around his neck. That would keep him cool for a while, at least until after chores were done.

Josiah carried the buckets a short distance to the main clearing. His family's cabin stood in the center of the clearing, with a small shed to one side that housed Father's prize oxen and a pair of goats. Chicken ranged freely near a crude coop. A row of stones formed a wall near the road that ran along the western side of the clearing. Beyond the shed were the fields, one for hay and one where shoots of corn stood in neat rows. Josiah looked proudly at the corn. He had broken the ground and planted it all himself. Even Grandfather said he couldn't have done better.

He went into the cabin, dim after the hazy sunshine. He set the buckets down on the dirt floor next to the stone hearth. His mother turned from her cooking.

"Fresh cream this morning, thanks to Nan," she said.

Josiah smiled. "And cheese, too, I hope."

"Stomachs," a voice came from the corner. "That's all you ever think of is your stomachs."

Josiah went to the bed that stood in one corner of the cabin. "Good morning, Grandfather. How are you?"

"How should I be?" the old man snapped. "Same as ever. Help me up."

Josiah helped the old man sit up and propped several pillows behind his back. "It will be another hot day. Mother and I will carry you out to the shade later. You will be cooler there."

Grandfather snorted. "Showing mercy to a crippled old man."

"Mr. Freeman! For shame, speaking that way," cried Mother. "I know you are bitter, but try to keep a civil tongue."

"And why shouldn't I be bitter? How would you like to lie here all day long with no legs to walk on?"

Mother handed him a bowl of porridge. "It was the Lord's will, you must believe that," she said gently. "Besides, I'm glad for the company during the day, and now you have time to carve. You have to admit you're earning good coin for your work."

The old man did not reply but spooned the porridge into his mouth.

Mother sighed and shook her head. Josiah caught her eye and shrugged his shoulders. It had been a difficult recovery for Grandfather, ever since a falling tree had smashed his legs earlier in the spring. Mother and Josiah had nursed him around the clock, but after several days it had become clear that more help was needed. Josiah had run through the night to bring Sarah Hawkins and her sister back. He assisted while the women performed the amputation.

He looked down at his porridge. "I don't think I'm hungry right now," he said to his mother. "I think I'll go work on the addition to the shed."

"All right," she said. "But if you want your porridge later, it will be cold. I'm damping down the fire. It will be hot enough today without it."

Josiah nodded. He put on his cap, grabbed his ax, and stepped outside. He walked over to the shed and stopped at the pile of logs that he and his father had cut the previous winter.

Father. I wonder where he is and what he's doing, thought Josiah. Is he even alive?

Matthew Freeman joined the Green Mountain Boys in 1775, when the colonies finally revolted against their British rulers. He left the farm in his own father's hands, returning home whenever there was a pause in the fighting. He had spent three months at home the previous winter.

Josiah loved to listen as Father and Grandfather swapped stories in front of the fire. Grandfather told of fighting the French and Indians in years past, while Father related stories of Fort Ticonderoga and naval battles on Lake Champlain. When Josiah voiced his longing to be a soldier, the older men laughed.

"You've got some growing to do first, boy," said Father, tousling his hair.

"I can do a full day's work in the fields," declared Josiah, "and I can handle the oxen."

"True enough," replied Father. "Still, the life of a soldier is too hard for a boy."

"Then if I can't be a soldier, can we get a horse? Then I could carry messages and take Mother visiting."

Father laughed. "Sounds like you have it all planned out. A horse is a big responsibility. I'll have to think on it."

Grandfather changed the subject, and no more mention was made of a horse, but Josiah worked hard all winter to show how responsible he really was.

Then in early April, the call went out again for the regiment to return to Ticonderoga. The Americans had been successful at the Battle of Princeton in early January, and now the news came out that the British were determined to beat their foes.

"This will be over soon, Anna," Father had said before leaving. "You're doing well without me. And the boy is old enough to help. In fact," he added, taking Josiah by the shoulder, "he's old enough to be building the stall for that horse he's been begging for."

Josiah's eyes lit up. Finally, his own horse! Even before Father was out of sight down the road, Josiah was hard at work on the new stall.

But tragedy struck in the form of the falling tree, and Josiah had taken over Grandfather's work in earnest, plowing and planting and clearing more land. The stall had to wait and now Josiah worried that he might not be able to finish it before Father's return.

If he returns, Josiah thought. The rumors flying up and down the road had not been good lately. Riders and traders spoke of a new British campaign in New York.

Rotten British, thought Josiah, striking the end of a log to cut a notch. Why can't they go home and leave us in peace?

The sound of hoofbeats on the road made Josiah look up. The horse and rider were in a hurry, by the sound of it, he thought.

The horse came into view. The rider was Sally Williams, and her two young children were clinging to her. Josiah ran to hold the horse.

"Raiders," she gasped, terror making her almost speechless. "Raiders are coming this way!"

— CHAPTER 3 —

Mother ran out of the cabin. "Sally, what is it?" she cried.

"Raiders are coming," Sally replied. The children clung to her and stared down at Josiah. Mother reached for Sally's hand and squeezed it. Her face was pale and strained.

"Which way?"

"Down from the north," Sally said, tears filling her eyes. "We barely got away. They're burning my cabin."

"Never mind about that, Sally. Cabins can be rebuilt. You just take care of those younguns. Where are you going?"

"Down to my sister's in Rutland. Zack stayed behind to do what he could. We never wanted any trouble. We just wanted to be left alone." Sally began to cry.

"Don't you worry now," said Mother, patting her on the arm. "Josiah, run and get that loaf of bread on the table." Josiah ran off. "What kind of raiders were they, Sally? Tories? British sympathizers?"

Sally nodded. "Tories and a few Injuns, not anyone I recognized," she said in a trembling voice. "They said something about Captain Sherwood."

"Sherwood," repeated Mother grimly. "He's Tory all right."

Josiah returned with the loaf of bread, and Mother thrust it into Sally's arms.

"There, it's all I've got. You hurry on now. Godspeed, Sally. I'll be looking for you when this is over."

Sally turned her horse and rode off, dust trailing behind.

"It's started," said Mother, hurrying back to the cabin. "The raiders will be after anything that's not nailed down. Josiah, you run all the stock into the woods as far as you can. Then come back and help me."

"But why don't we hitch the oxen to the wagon and leave?" asked Josiah.

"They're too slow. The raiders would catch up with us and take the oxen and the wagon," she replied. "We're better off staying and hiding what we can."

Josiah nodded in agreement and ran off. Besides, he told himself, I'll fight them off!

Josiah led the oxen out of their shed and into the trees. They moved slowly, no matter how hard Josiah tugged on their halters. He finally reached a small clearing that he hoped was far enough away from the cabin. The oxen had left a trail, but maybe the raiders would be in too much of a hurry to notice it. He returned to the shed, untied the goats, Billy and Nan, and shooed them into the woods. The chickens needed no urging and scattered before him.

Josiah ran back to the cabin. Mother had stripped the beds of the linens and thrust a bundle into his arms.

"Go hide this," she said. "And don't stuff it under a thornbush."

Josiah ran back into the woods and hid the bundle in some tall weeds. As he returned, Mother hurried out with her cooking pot and kettle. She handed them to Josiah.

"Put these in the hidey-hole."

Josiah ran into the woods a short way to a pile of boulders. This was Mother's hidey-hole, as she called it. He removed one large rock, then another, until he had a large enough opening. Then he thrust the kettle and pot into the deep cavity. When he replaced the rocks, no one could have guessed that there was anything underneath.

Josiah grinned. He and Father had teased Mother about her hidey-hole, but now it meant the difference between losing everything and being able to survive.

When he returned to the cabin, Mother was on her knees near the brook, digging a hole.

"Grandmother's teapot," she said shortly, and placed a delicate bone china teapot into the hole. She smoothed the dirt over it and looked around.

"Put that old log over it," she directed Josiah. "Make it look like there's nothing there."

Mother went to the shed. She picked up Josiah's ax, where he had laid it when Sally Williams rode up. He watched, horrified, as she began slashing at the wagon.

"What are you doing?"

"We can always repair the wagon after the raiders leave, but if they find it in one piece, they'll take it!"

Josiah marveled at his mother's reasoning. He joined in, removing a wheel and breaking the spokes. The iron rim rolled into the woods.

He went back to his mother. She picked up some dirt and rubbed it into her dress. "Dirty yourself, then," she said. "We want the raiders to think we're poor so they won't start looking for our food."

Josiah nodded and rubbed dirt into the face he had just washed. Then he rolled around on the ground, smiling for a moment at his mother's look of dismay.

"I'll never get those clothes clean," she said.

Josiah and Mother returned to the cabin. It had been almost stripped bare of their few possessions. Mother left their oldest clothes hanging on the wall. The only other things remaining were the mattresses, beds, and the long table. And Grandfather in his bed.

Mother picked up the musket and handed it to Grandfather. "Can you sit on it?" she asked. "I can't let the raiders get it."

"Aren't we going to stand and fight?" cried Josiah.

"No, there will be too many of them. We can only hope they won't bother with us."

"You can't stay here, woman," said Grandfather. "You take the boy and hide. I'll be all right."

"No," said Mother firmly. "I'll not leave you here alone. There's no telling what the raiders might do. But you, Josiah, you can go into the woods."

Josiah shook his head. "No, I won't leave, either."

"Sh!" hissed Grandfather. "I hear something." The three stood still and listened. "Looks like nobody's getting away now," said Grandfather. "Sounds like they're coming!"

—CHAPTER 4—

Mother and Josiah ran to the door and looked out.

A group of men was coming down the road from the north. They led a few horses, and a small herd of cattle followed in the distance.

There were about twenty men in all, and as they got closer, Josiah saw that a few of them were dressed only in buckskins and had most of their hair shaved off. Indians! Mohawk Indians! Josiah gaped at them. He had seen natives before, back in Massachusetts, but he had only heard frightening stories of these fierce northern warriors.

Mother squared her shoulders, clenched her fists by her sides, and stepped out to meet them. The group halted in the road. One of the white men came forward. He was dirty and unshaven, and an ugly scar marred his face.

"Good day, mistress," the man said, tilting his hat slightly. "How do you do?"

Mother did not reply, and as Josiah moved to her side, he was shocked to see blazing anger in her face.

"We're buying food for the soldiers, ma'am," he said, coming closer.

"And what soldiers might that be?" asked Mother between tight lips.

"Why, His Majesty's loyal troops, of course."

"We have nothing to sell," replied Mother.

The man motioned to the group, and they moved in closer. Josiah took a step toward Mother, and she put her arms around his shoulder. He felt her trembling but could detect no sign of fear in either her voice or her expression.

"Surely you have something you can share," the man said. "We'll pay for it," he added, fingering a pouch at his waist. He looked around the clearing. "A place like this must have some cattle."

"We sold our cow last spring for seed. The goats got eaten by a wolf."

"And I suppose a fox got the chickens," the man sneered.

"Just this morning," said Mother with icy calm.

"Well, that's too bad," he snapped, stepping closer. "You know what happens to those who interfere with His Majesty's troops? They get their property confiscated!"

Mother glared at him in reply. He waved his men forward. "Burn it," he said.

"No!" cried Mother, stepping forward. "My father-in-law is in there!"

"Then make him come out. What is he, some kind of coward, that he lets his women speak for him?" He strode to the cabin, Mother and Josiah close behind.

"No, he's crippled," she said. "Leave him alone. He's suffered enough."

A bellow of rage greeted them as they stepped into the dark cabin.

"I'm no coward, you unspeakable varmint!" Grandfather was sitting up in bed, eyes blazing, white hair standing on end like the halo of an avenging angel. "I am a captain in His Majesty's Third Rangers, and I have more bravery in my little toe than all of you put together. Come over here, and I'll beat you into the ground!" He raised his arms and beat at the air. He whooped and hollered and foamed at the mouth. Josiah watched in horror.

The scarred man looked at the bed where the flat blanket showed that Grandfather had no legs. Josiah held his breath. Would he find the musket?

One of the Mohawks had padded silently into the cabin and now went over to the scarred man.

"The old man—not right in his head," he said to his companion. "Don't hurt him, my people say, his spirit will follow us."

The scarred man looked at Grandfather and then at the Indian.

"All right, but we have to have something for our trouble." He turned to Mother, and she stepped back, holding Josiah to her.

18

"Don't hurt woman," said the Indian. "General won't pay if we hurt white women."

"What about the boy, then?"

Josiah took a deep breath as the Indian walked over and took him by the arm. He stood motionless as the man studied his face.

Josiah gulped for air. He could see nothing but dark eyes staring into his. Then suddenly the Indian released him, pushing him away.

"No good for slave," he said. "Young boys eat too much, work too little." His eyes traveled over the walls of the cabin until he spotted Mother's second-best dress hanging on a peg. He lifted it down. "Take this," he said, and left.

The scarred man looked back at Grandfather, who had quieted down and now sat rocking back and forth, humming off key.

"His Majesty's Third Rangers, did you say? Does that mean you're loyal? Will you swear an oath of loyalty to the king?"

"Aye, Third Rangers," said Grandfather. "Where are those rotten Frenchmen? Let me at them! Corporal"—he pointed to Josiah—"send word that we're surrounded. We'll fight them to the last man!" He began to punch at the air again, fighting the enemies of his youth, reliving the battles of the French and Indian Wars.

Mother said, "He's been like this since the accident. Please go, and leave us be."

The man looked at Mother and Josiah. "All right, for his sake," he motioned to Grandfather. "For the sake of an old soldier. But I know you are rebels." He shook his finger at Mother. "You are rebels, and you are going to pay!" With that, he stalked out of the cabin.

Mother sank to the floor with a deep sigh and rested her head against Grandfather's bed.

"Thanks be to God," she breathed. "You saved us. That was quite a performance."

Grandfather lay back and closed his eyes. "Aye, for a minute there I almost convinced myself I was crazy."

Josiah looked at the two of them. "You mean, you were acting?"

Grandfather opened one eye. "Aye, boy. Most folks keep their distance from crazy people. I didn't want them coming over here and finding our only gun."

"At least they're gone," said Mother. They listened as the raiders moved off down the road, their shouts finally dying off. But then Josiah heard another sound, the crackling of fire.

He raced out the door. The shed was engulfed in flames. He ran to the water trough, but it had been smashed. The log pipeline was destroyed, and he looked on helplessly as the roof of the shed fell in, sending up a shower of sparks. He backed away from the heat, and Mother came out and put her arm around him. They watched silently as the shed tumbled into a blazing bonfire.

He looked out to his trampled cornfield, and his eyes misted. All that work, ruined for no good reason.

Mother hugged him. "It looks like we've got our work cut out for us." She looked into Josiah's eyes. "The life of a farmer is always a battle. The raiders hurt us, but we'll rebuild and replant. That's what farmers do. They won't win unless we let them."

Josiah nodded and picked up the pieces of a wooden bucket. "What if they come back?"

"I doubt they will. But if raiders are about, that means the army is on the move." She looked thoughtful and worried, then she smiled and turned to Josiah. "Let's not worry about trouble till it finds us. In the meantime, let's get to work."

— CHAPTER 5 —

Hubbardton, Vermont
July 6, 1777 Afternoon

It was a long hot march from Mount Independence. The memory of the evacuation quickly blurred in Captain Johnson's mind, but he and his men had exchanged only a few shots with the enemy. They had expected to be chased out of Mount Independence, but there had been no close pursuit by the Germans or British after the brief skirmish.

Captain Johnson and Matthew Freeman pondered this as they stopped for a short rest.

"They probably stopped to re-equip themselves," said Matthew. "We left a lot of stores behind."

"Re-equip? You mean plunder," replied Captain Johnson. "Whatever the reason, I'm glad they weren't right on our heels. It would have been a running fight all the way."

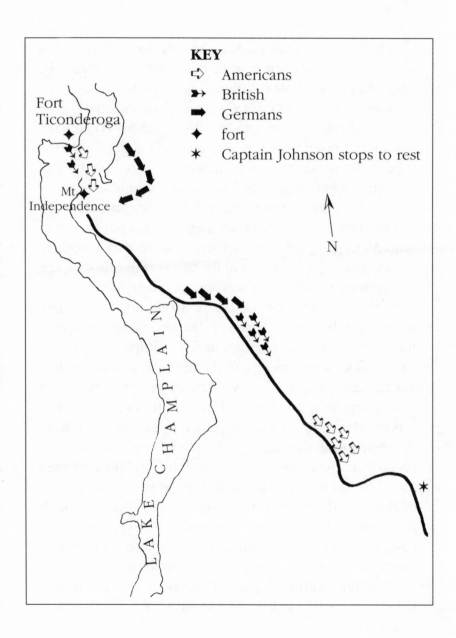

KEY
⇨ Americans
➤➤ British
➡ Germans
◆ fort
✱ Captain Johnson stops to rest

Fort
Ticonderoga

Mt.
Independence

N

LAKE CHAMPLAIN

Matthew Freeman nodded and stood up. "Speaking of which, I don't care to wait here and show them the way." Captain Johnson grunted agreement and ordered his men to their feet. "Let's go, men," he called.

It was stiflingly hot. It had been hot for days, each day more humid than the last, and the forest did little to relieve it. In addition, the mosquitoes and biting flies near the boggy areas were almost unendurable.

Colonel Francis moved up and down the lines throughout the day, encouraging his men and keeping them in line. As Captain Johnson helped herd up the stragglers, he felt a growing admiration for this young officer. Even the most exhausted man was spurred on by a word from him. "It's amazing that he is able to get this number of men to go this far in these conditions," thought Captain Johnson. "That is a true sign of leadership."

At midday, scouts reported that the British were closing in again, supported by German troops. They even sent a messenger to Colonel Francis to suggest he surrender. His reply was to simply urge his men on faster.

By the time they had reached the settlements at Hubbardton in midafternoon, Captain Johnson knew his men could go no further. He paused as he reached the crest of the hill. Before him the road twisted down through the trees and crossed a small brook. Beyond the brook rose a hill, where he could already make out the beginnings of a camp. A sentry ran to meet him.

"Colonel Warner requests that you take your men to the west side of the hill, sir," he said. "You are to make camp there."

Captain Johnson nodded wearily. "And General St. Clair?"

"He has moved on to Castle Town and left Colonel Warner in charge here. The colonel has decided not to go any farther today."

"Thank goodness for that," replied the captain. The sentry saluted and stepped aside as the captain led his men down the road. They stopped to fill their waterskins at the brook and then moved on to the hillside.

Matthew Freeman caught up to Captain Johnson as he brought his men up from the rear. "The sick have gone with Captain Carr to the west of the camp," he said. "Reports are that the British are several miles back." He looked up at the distant ridge.

"You're almost home, aren't you?" said Captain Johnson.

"Right over that ridge," Matthew replied.

"Too bad you can't go visit," said Captain Johnson.

"That will have to wait. My duty is here with these men. Still, I'd like to see if Pa got a good crop of corn going," he said wistfully.

Captain Johnson laughed and slapped him on the back. "Always a farmer."

Matthew smiled. "Yep, but I'm enough of a soldier to appreciate Colonel Warner's stopping here. This is probably the best place to camp between here and Castle Town. There's a good view of the approaching enemy, and the hill is easier to defend."

"Do you think there will be a fight?" asked Captain Johnson.

"I hope not, but I think there might be," replied Matthew grimly. "And I'll wager that is what the colonel is thinking too."

The two units arranged themselves on the hillside. They cut down trees and dragged them to the edge of the camp and laid them side by side with the branches pointing out. This crude *abatis* would not stop the enemy, but it would slow them down.

The men ate their supper and then settled down for the night. The captains were summoned to a nearby farmhouse to meet with Colonel Warner and the rest of the officers.

"Rest while you can," Captain Johnson told his men before he left. "This isn't over yet."

— Chapter 6 —

Pittsford, Vermont
July 7, 1777 Daybreak

Josiah woke to the sound of thunder. Must be a storm, he thought, rubbing his eyes. Sounds like hail too.

But as his eyes focused, he saw sunshine seeping through the cracks in the log walls.

"That can't be a storm!" he exclaimed. "It must be—it must be guns!"

He heard Mother moving around below, and he called out, "Mother, it's fighting!"

She appeared at the foot of the ladder to Josiah's sleeping loft. "I think it's over the ridge," she said.

Josiah threw on his clothes and scrambled down. He would have run out of the cabin, but Mother placed a hand on his arm.

"Slow down, boy. You can't see anything from here. You have chores to do before you go running off. Here"—she thrust a bowl into his hands—"eat this and then go

27

look for the oxen again. Maybe they just wandered off. The raiders must have missed something yesterday."

The gunfire was sporadic. At each new burst, Mother jumped.

"That sounds close," said Josiah. "Do you think they'll come this way?"

"Maybe, but I doubt it. The ridge is pretty steep, and they're probably headed for Castle Town," said Mother. "You never mind that shooting and eat your porridge." Tension made her voice sharp.

Grandfather fidgeted in the corner. "Sure is hard for a body to stay still with all that shooting going on. What I wouldn't give to be able to go take a look-see."

"I know," said Mother, "but we're safer here. Josiah, there might be some chickens left in the woods. If they're scared from the shooting, they'll find someplace to roost. Look for them while you're out there. And don't go far," she said as Josiah nodded and stepped out of the door.

The shooting sounded louder, and Josiah felt exposed standing in the clearing. He quickly made his way to the trees and looked back.

Smoke still hung in the air where the shed smoldered. The sun was just coming up over the trees behind the cabin, but it was already hot.

He crossed the road where he had chased the animals the day before. Just as he was about to step into the trees, he heard hoofbeats coming down the road. He dove into the undergrowth and peered out, his heart hammering. Had the raiders come back? His tongue stuck in his dry mouth as he tried to call out to warn Mother.

A single horse appeared around the bend. The rider reined in as he approached the clearing, and Josiah saw his face clearly. Relieved, he ran out of his hiding place.

"Mr. Hardy, Mr. Hardy," he called, running to hold the horse as the man dismounted. "What is happening?"

"They're fighting over near Selleck's in Hubbardton. The British have attacked our troops."

"But they're at Fort Ticonderoga!" cried Mother, hurrying out of the cabin.

"Fort Ti's been taken, ma'am," Mr. Hardy said. "Our boys were retreating down toward Fort Edward, and the British caught up with the rear guard this morning."

"And Seth Warner's men?" asked Mother.

"They were part of the rear guard, ma'am," he replied.

"My Matthew," said Mother. "My Matthew is with Seth Warner. He's over there fighting right now." She looked westward to the high ridge.

"Looks like you've had your troubles here too," said Mr. Hardy. "Raiders?"

Mother nodded. "Yesterday."

"They were sent out by the British to scout the area. They burned the Williamses' cabin and mine." He waved away Mother's sympathy. "I didn't lose much. My Martha's down in Boston with her mother. The raiders didn't burn your cabin, though."

Mother shook her head. "We couldn't move Matthew's father, so we stayed. He acted like a crazy man and spooked them."

Mr. Hardy smiled. "He's a sly old fox. I wouldn't want to tangle with him, crippled or not."

29

"Will the soldiers come this way, sir?" asked Josiah eagerly.

"Hard to tell. You'd best be ready to leave, though. The raiders might come back," he said. "I'm off to warn the rest of the folks. Most everybody's leaving, Miz Freeman. You'd best think about going away too."

Mother shook her head. "We have worked too hard to go off and leave our home now. I'd rather take my chances with the raiders again."

Mr. Hardy nodded and turned toward the road. "Now we pay for our independence," he called as he rode off.

"So," said Mother. "Matthew's just on the other side of the ridge. If only we knew what was happening!" She bit her lip and looked anxiously toward the ridge again. Another volley of shots sounded. She turned to Josiah. "Do you think you can go up top and look around without getting hurt?"

Josiah's face lit up. "Yes."

"But don't go too near. Just stay long enough to see what's going on. I need you safe," she said, taking him by the shoulders.

"I'll be careful," Josiah reassured her. "I know my way through the woods."

"Go then," said Mother. "Come right back if you see anyone coming this way."

Josiah saluted her and ran to the other side of the road. He waved briefly at his mother, then ducked down the path.

Josiah and his father had walked to Hubbardton the year before. He knew Selleck's cabin lay roughly to the west of his. There was a path that led directly over Pittsford Ridge, as the dividing ridge was called, but Josiah decided against taking it. It might land him right in the middle of the fighting.

The path rose sharply in front of him, and he turned right, to the north, down a smaller, almost invisible path. This path had been made by animals, but Josiah knew it circled around Pittsford Ridge. He would end up near the source of a small brook and north of the Selleck cabin.

They've probably taken the new military road from Fort Ti, thought Josiah. The road goes right below Sargent Hill. That would be a good place to attack any pursuers. He thought about the layout of Selleck's farm. The pasture on the hill would have a good view of anyone coming from the north. No wonder Colonel Warner had camped there.

Josiah moved swiftly up the tiny path. Animals almost always find the easiest path through the trees, and this one was fairly smooth. Josiah paused for moment and listened.

The battle sounded farther away, as he had expected. The forest was silent. The birds and squirrels and insects were motionless, waiting for the strange far-off sounds that signaled danger to cease.

Crack! A twig snapped near the path ahead of him. Josiah froze.

Something was coming through the trees!

Josiah edged over to a large tree. Must be an animal, he thought. Even a man doesn't make that much noise.

But what kind of animal? A bear, maybe even a wolverine?

Josiah waited. He held his breath and his heart pounded. Just as he was about to swing himself up into the tree, the animal burst through the bushes.

It was Billy! Josiah laughed out loud from relief. The goat stopped and looked at Josiah, tilting his head comically.

"Am I glad to see you, you old goat!" said Josiah. "I should have known you'd be smart enough to stay away from those raiders. You go home now." Josiah led Billy down the path a short way. "You go home."

Josiah released Billy and pushed him. "Go on," he repeated. Billy turned to follow Josiah. "No, go home," he shouted. He picked up a rock and threw it at the stubborn goat.

"I've got more important things to do than to take you home," he said. He stooped for another rock, and Billy finally understood. He turned and ran down the path.

Josiah watched as the goat disappeared through the trees, then he turned and continued on his journey.

— CHAPTER 7 —

Hubbardton, Vermont
July 7, 1777

Captain Johnson crouched behind the stone wall and reloaded. The British were making another advance up the hill, but the smoke hung in the hot air and visibility was poor. His eyes watered and his lungs burned as he took aim. Noise filled his ears until he could finally hear nothing except the pounding of his own heart. He squeezed the trigger, and the recoil jerked him back. He dropped to the ground to reload again without even looking to see if he had hit his target.

Time seemed to stand still as the battle raged. The Americans fought back furiously as the British came on. At one point, they had almost broken the British line, but then a fresh unit of redcoats marched in from the west. They reformed and renewed their attack on the hill where the Americans fired from behind a stone wall.

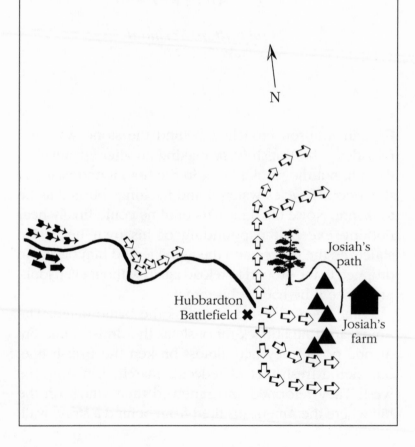

A courier raced up behind the captain. He saw him mouth the order, "Colonel Warner says to retreat as planned." He nodded, and the courier dashed off to the next unit.

Captain Johnson relayed the order to his sergeant, and he passed it on. The men stopped firing one by one and, crouching low, ran down the hill to the other side of a small rise.

"Remember," the captain told his men, "hold them as long as you can behind the fence. When the signal is given, retreat south to Manchester as best you can. Go over the ridge if you have to."

The British surged over the stone wall. "Go!" he yelled, and the men raced to the protection of a high log fence in the shadow of the ridge above.

Captain Johnson waited to bring up the rear, then followed his men. As he ran, something hit him hard on the back of his shoulder. The impact threw him forward, and he crashed to his knees.

"I'm hit," he thought with surprise as he went down. He put a hand to his shoulder and watched in wonder as blood oozed between his fingers. He swayed on his knees, struggling to stay in control, but a black curtain seemed to come down around his head. He fell to the ground, and just as he lost consciousness, he thought he heard music—trumpets blaring, fifes rippling, and drums beating, beating, beating. . . .

— CHAPTER 8 —

By midmorning, Josiah had circled around the north end of the ridge. He climbed a tree and looked out.

He was in a small cleft, formed by Pittsford Ridge on his left and a smaller hill on his right. Straight ahead stood Sargent Hill, and he knew that down below the road wound through the trees.

The distant mountains faded in a curtain of haze. The heat shimmered in front of Josiah's eyes. He listened for a moment.

At first he could not hear much. A large insect whipped past, and Josiah sat very still. Then he heard it—a low throbbing noise, a far-off roar, the sound of thousands of men caught in the grip of battle.

Josiah's heart beat faster. He was getting close to the fighting, but still he could see nothing but a little smoke hanging over the ridge to his left. He decided to get closer.

He crept from tree to tree. The sound of gunfire got louder as he went, and soon he could make out the sounds of the individual shots. But there was something else, too, and as he crept the low roar turned into yelling and drumbeats and screaming.

He chose a tall tree and climbed carefully, making sure that the leaves would hide him. He knew that he was close to the fighting now.

Josiah crawled down a branch and looked out. He gasped and clung to the branch as the sight below unfolded. He saw men shooting guns and men falling and men crawling in agony. He heard the shots and watched as men fell screaming, and he too felt pain cut through him.

He closed his eyes and gulped in large breaths of air. Then he looked out again, forcing himself to study the scene.

Most of the shooting was taking place to his left. There was a cornfield at the bottom of the ridge and a tall log fence to the west of it. Most of the uniforms that he saw were red or blue. Where were the soldiers in rough buckskin, the Americans?

Josiah closed his hand into a tube. He squinted through it with one eye, forming a telescope.

Those are British soldiers, he thought. They've chased the Americans to this side of that log fence, and now they're all going up the ridge. But it's too steep. Our men will never get away from them! They're cut off!

Josiah heard a bugle and saw a detachment of redcoats run up the rocks into the trees. They were hidden from view, but Josiah heard the volley of shots. Our men are on the ridge, he thought, tightening a fist, and they're fighting back! Oh, if only I had a gun, I could get them too!

But then Josiah looked back at the battlefield and saw all the fallen men. His stomach tightened, and he swallowed. Would he really be able to do that to another man?

The shooting suddenly sounded closer, and smoke stung his eyes. Josiah jumped as a musket ball thudded into a tree nearby. He crouched, stunned.

I'd better get out of here, he thought. I have to tell Mother that the soldiers might be coming up the ridge. She'll have my hide if I get myself shot!

He swung himself out of the tree. Taking care to stay in thick cover, he cautiously went back the way he had come. The sounds receded as he went, but still he heard the low roar. He ran through a small clearing to the home-ward path.

As he jumped a small brook, he heard a sound close behind him. The soldiers! They were headed right for him!

It was too late to hide. Josiah froze.

A figure thrust into sight, weaving and stumbling. As it got closer, Josiah realized that this was no musket-wielding soldier—it was a boy! He wore a bright yellow and blue uniform, now bloodstained and tattered.

Scattered thoughts ran through Josiah's mind. Had he come to see the battle too and gotten shot? Who could he be?

The boy saw Josiah. "No shoot," he gasped, waving his arms. "No gun, no shoot!" He rocked back and forth and then slowly dropped to his knees. "Help," he whispered as he sank unconscious to the ground.

Josiah hesitated, but then ran to the sprawled figure. He held out a shaking hand and gently touched the boy. "Wake up," he said. There was no response.

Josiah gulped. What should he do? He remembered the horror of Grandfather's smashed legs, but Mother had been there to take charge and tell him what to do. What if this boy should die right here in front of him?

Under the blood, the boy's face had a strange gray look. He was breathing slowly, but although his uniform was spattered with blood, his arms and legs appeared unharmed. Josiah gently turned the boy's head. Blood was oozing from a wound right above the ear.

Josiah took off his neckerchief and ran to the nearby brook. He dipped the cloth in the cold water and returned to kneel beside the boy.

He gently dabbed at the blood that covered the side of the boy's head. His skin was still pale beneath the blood and dirt, but he seemed to be breathing easier. Josiah bathed him again, and the touch of the cool water roused the boy and his eyes fluttered.

"Help," he gasped again, his blue eyes opening wide with fright. He murmured and struggled to get up.

"Who are you?" asked Josiah, helping him sit up. "Are you English?"

"*Englisch*? Not *Englisch*. *Braunschweig*, I am *Braunschweig*." The boy tried to stand up, but he tottered, and

Josiah led him to a boulder to sit down. The head wound had begun to bleed again, and Josiah pressed his kerchief against it.

"Whoever you are, you need help," said Josiah.

"*Ja,* help," repeated the boy. "Army, where? Lost army." He looked around, dazed.

He sure is lost, Josiah said to himself. Now what am I going to do? Here I am, a long way from home, in a war with a wounded boy who definitely does not belong here. He must be one of those Germans the redcoats got to help them. "German?" he said to the boy.

"*Ja,* German," replied the boy. "Lost army, lost army."

"I suppose that makes you my prisoner," said Josiah. "But what should I do with you?"

The boy looked up at Josiah, blinking. He was still pale, and his eyes were glazed.

"I suppose I could leave you here and hope someone finds you." Josiah looked at the drooping figure. "No, I can't be sure they would find you this far from the fighting. And you'd never make your way back without help."

"Help?" the boy said.

"Yes, I'll help you. Come," Josiah said, stooping and putting the boy's arm around his shoulder. He helped him stand up. "I'll take you to Mother. She'll know what to do."

"*Mutter?*" The boy began mumbling in his own language, but he allowed Josiah to lead him away.

The going was slow, because the boy could not walk on his own. Josiah picked his way around the ridge carefully. They stopped and rested often, and each time the boy sank to the ground.

The trees barely rustled as the sun rose in the sky. It was very hot, and there was no breeze to cool them. Under the canopy of trees, it was shady, but the flies and mosquitoes tormented them.

Josiah and the boy came to a small stream. Josiah knelt and dug up clumps of mud. He smeared it thickly over his face and then turned to the boy.

"It's all right," he said as the boy shrank back. "It will keep the flies away." The boy stared and shook his head.

Josiah flapped his arms. "Buzz-z-z, flies, buzz-z-z. . . ."

The boy nodded in understanding. Josiah covered the boy's head wound thickly with mud, then applied it to his face and neck. He helped the boy to his feet, and they continued on their way.

Progress was slow, and several times Josiah had to help the boy crawl down the boulders that formed the ridge. After what seemed like hours, they reached the spot where Josiah had seen Billy. There was no sign of the goat now.

"At least we're almost home now," said Josiah. And not too soon, he thought as he looked at the boy, who had gone limp and lay gasping.

One last time Josiah shouldered the boy and they stumbled through the trees. As they neared the cabin, Josiah began shouting for Mother.

They stepped out onto the road, and Mother ran to meet them.

"What's all the shouting? What's this?" she cried. "Why, it's a soldier! And just a boy!"

"I found him wandering in the woods near the battle," said Josiah. "I didn't know what to do with him."

Mother put her arm around the boy. "You'll be fine," she said. "You're safe. I'll take care of you."

The boy smiled weakly, then his head lolled as he again lost consciousness.

"Let's get him inside," said Mother. The two lifted the boy and carried him to the cabin.

"Lay him here on my bed," directed Mother.

"What's this?" demanded Grandfather. "What's going on?"

"It's a boy, Grandfather. I found him wandering in the woods. He's hurt."

"Looks like a soldier. One of the enemy," said Grandfather. "You're giving aid to the enemy, woman."

"Hush, Mr. Freeman. Can't you see he's hurt? Josiah, fresh water and the bandages and my medicine bag from the hidey-hole," she ordered as she rolled up her sleeves.

Josiah grabbed the buckets and darted out the door. He raced to the hidey-hole and found the bag. He threw it across his shoulder and ran back to the brook for water.

He hurried into the cabin where Mother was stripping the boy of his bloody uniform. In the corner, Grandfather still grumbled.

"Mr. Freeman, I would not turn away King George himself if he needed help, so stop your mouth right now," Mother snapped. "Besides, I don't think this boy is English. The uniform is different."

"He said he's German," said Josiah. "He doesn't speak English very well."

"Bah, Germans," spat Grandfather. "Mercenaries, paid murderers is what they are."

"You hush now. This boy is no murderer," Mother replied. "Josiah, help me here."

Josiah assisted her, and soon they had the boy bathed and resting between clean sheets.

Mother turned her attention to the head wound. She cleaned it of the mud that Josiah had applied. It was no longer bleeding, so she pressed some leaves from her medicine bag against it. Then she bound it firmly with a long piece of linen.

"We'll need more water," she said to Josiah. "We'll keep bathing him until he gets cooler. I think he has a touch of sunstroke as well as the head wound."

"Will he be all right?" asked Josiah.

"I think so. He should come out of this faint soon. As long as that wound does not fester, it should heal easily."

Josiah returned to the brook and refilled the buckets. As he approached the cabin, he heard someone shouting.

"Halloo, halloo" came the cry.

Josiah ducked into the cabin. "Someone's coming!" he cried.

— CHAPTER 9 —

Mother grabbed the musket and ran to the door, Josiah close behind. "If it's raiders, we'll have to stand and fight," she said grimly.

A man stepped slowly from the trees and leaned on his musket. "Eb Hawkins!" gasped Mother, handing the musket to Josiah. "You were with Matthew! What's happened?" She ran to meet him.

"We almost held them off," he said as Mother led him to a boulder in the shade to rest. "We would have held the hill if the blasted Germans hadn't come." He sat wearily, and Mother motioned for Josiah to fetch water.

"Our orders were to delay the British as long as we could so the main army could get away," said Mr. Hawkins as he splashed water on his face. "Colonel Warner figured Selleck's place would be easy to defend. We held them off all right," continued Mr. Hawkins. He paused to drink deeply of the cool water.

"But then the Germans came marching down from the north. They sounded like Judgment Day, with all those horns blowing. They ripped right into the Eleventh Massachusetts regiment and killed Colonel Francis. The redcoats cut us off to the south, so Warner sent us up the ridge and told us to regroup near Manchester."

"But, Matthew, what about Matthew?" Mother's eyes begged for news.

"As far as I know, he's fine. I was pushed up this way, but the rest of them went toward the south. I'm sorry," he added. "I wish I could tell you for sure."

Mother sighed deeply and closed her eyes. "If he made it to the ridge, he'll be all right." She opened her eyes and stood up. "Now, then, all I can offer you is some cold porridge and hardtack. And it's a great deal cooler out here than in the cabin. Josiah," she called, "fetch Mr. Hawkins some food."

Josiah went into the cabin. The German boy still lay quietly, and Grandfather muttered in his corner.

"Who's out there?" he asked.

"Mr. Hawkins from Pittsford way," said Josiah. "He was in the fighting. He says Father's all right."

"Thank God for that," said Grandfather. "What about your friend here?" he said, motioning to the boy. "Are you going to tell him about that?"

"I don't know," said Josiah.

"Looks mighty suspicious," said the old man. "The

cabin not being burned by the Tories, and now this boy lying here as guest of honor."

Josiah flushed. "Mr. Hawkins knows we're patriots." He spooned some porridge into a wooden bowl and took some small hard biscuits out of a barrel.

"Still, folks might wonder," called Grandfather as Josiah left.

Josiah carried the meager meal to Mr. Hawkins. Grandfather had a point. Should they tell Mr. Hawkins about the boy?

Mother took the food from him. "How's Grandfather?" she said, looking him hard in the eye. "I think you better go sit with him."

Josiah caught her meaning. "Oh, yes," he said. "I'll go and sit with him."

"Is Mr. Freeman ill?" asked Mr. Hawkins.

"He was injured a couple of months ago. Sometimes he starts raving about enemies in the cabin. I didn't want to worry Matthew about it. You won't tell him, will you?"

"Oh, no, ma'am. Is there anything I can do?"

Josiah went into the cabin as his mother answered, "Oh, that's very kind of you, but we can manage."

"So she won't tell him," said Grandfather. "Smart woman, your mother. But you better decide what you're going to do with that boy."

Josiah nodded. He replaced the wet cloth on the boy's forehead. "I guess I really complicated things, bringing him here," he said. "But I couldn't leave him out there to die."

Grandfather grunted. "I suppose you're right," he admitted. "But this is war, and folks don't always do what's right by their neighbor."

Josiah went to the door. Mr. Hawkins stood up and handed his bowl to Mother.

"I can't spare the time to go home," he said. "Can you get word through to Sarah? Give her my love, and tell her, well—tell her I think of her and the children every minute."

"Certainly." Mother smiled. "Godspeed, Mr. Hawkins."

Mr. Hawkins nodded to Josiah and Mother and set off down the road. He turned at the bend and waved, and then he was gone.

Mother sighed deeply.

"What would he have said if he knew we had a German here in our cabin?" asked Josiah.

"Surely he would not blame us for taking care of a wounded boy," said Mother as they went into the cabin. "Still, we do have a problem."

Mother bent over the boy and felt his cheek. As she did so, his eyes fluttered open. He looked around and struggled to sit up as he took in his surroundings.

"No, lie down," Mother said kindly. "You will be fine. You are safe." She paused and said, "*Sicher.*" At that the boy sank back.

"*Danke,*" he whispered. A torrent of German followed, but Mother shook her head.

"*Nein,* I only know a few words. What is your name?"

"Ah, name," the boy repeated. "Hans. Hans Klein."

"I didn't know you could speak German," interrupted Josiah.

"I can't. I learned a few words from a neighbor once, but that is all. Of course, many of our words are the same," replied Mother.

The boy watched them intently as they spoke. "Name?" he said, pointing to them.

"Josiah," said Mother, putting a hand on her son's arm. Then she pointed to herself. "Frau Freeman."

"Freedom? Ah, *Freiheit*, freedom," the boy said with a smile.

"No, Freeman," said Mother. "We are fighting for freedom."

The boy nodded slightly, but the brief conversation had tired him out, and he drifted off to sleep.

"We won't be free men for long if that enemy soldier is found here," said Grandfather from the corner.

Mother sighed. "He's just a boy. He wouldn't hurt us."

"I wonder what he's doing here. He's my age, or even younger," said Josiah. "I'm not old enough to fight, but he's not only in the army, he's thousands of miles from home."

"Them Germans teach their boys to fight young. Most of them are professional soldiers all their lives. They go wherever there's a fight and folks are willing to pay," said Grandfather.

Mother replaced the compress on Hans's head. "Thousands of miles away is a German woman wondering if her son is well," she said quietly.

Josiah heard a noise and turned toward the open doorway. There was a bleat, then Billy stepped into view.

"Billy!" Josiah cried. "So you finally came home!"

Josiah ran outside, and there stood not just Billy, but Nan too. She stood with her head drooping, her udder miserably full.

Mother's face lit up. "Now I can give Hans some milk! That should put him right."

Josiah tied Billy and Nan to a tree near the cabin while Mother milked the unhappy goat.

"At least we've got the goats back," she said with a smile. "Things are looking up!"

—CHAPTER 10—

The rest of the afternoon dragged by slowly. Occasionally a shot rang out in the distance, but the battle appeared to be over.

Mother and Josiah took turns sitting with Hans as he drifted in and out of sleep. Grandfather sat in his corner and whittled, muttering under his breath. The forced inactivity did not suit him well at all.

While Mother sat with Hans, Josiah went outside and worked on a temporary shelter for the goats. He cut small saplings and stuck them in the ground side by side. He wove them together with strong vines and covered the crude shelter with pine boughs.

When he was finished, he returned to the cabin. Hans was awake and sitting up.

Mother smiled. "Our patient is very well. I think the

long sleep was what he needed most. Now I think he could use some food."

Josiah sat down at his side. "How is your head?" he asked, pointing to his own head.

"Bad head," said Hans.

"How did you get hurt? Were you in the battle?"

"Battle?"

Josiah held up an imaginary gun and fired it. "Boom!" he said.

Hans's face cleared. "Ah, *ja*, battle. I play *Trommel*." He beat his hands on his legs. *"Trommel, ja?"*

Josiah nodded. "Drum. You are a drummer boy?"

Hans nodded quickly. *"Trompete,* fall, I fall, rock on head. Lost *Trommel,"* he added sadly.

Mother returned to his side with a bowl of warm milk. Hans drank it quickly and wiped his face with the back of his hand.

Mother felt his forehead. "No fever," she said. She rummaged in her medicine bag and drew out a piece of bark. "Chew this," she said, handing it to Hans. "It will help your head."

"He says he's a drummer boy," said Josiah.

"I thought he was too young to be a soldier," said Mother.

"Soldier or not," said Grandfather, "he's still the enemy. What are you going to do with him?"

"He could stay here," said Josiah. "After all, he is my prisoner. We could say he's my cousin, as long as he keeps his mouth shut. He would be a hard worker,

51

I know. And you always said it was a shame there was no one nearby to be my friend."

"How would we hide him every time someone came by?" asked Mother. "This road is becoming more and more traveled."

"You can't keep the enemy in your house just because you want a friend," said Grandfather. "Besides, every soldier's first duty when he's captured is to escape and go back to his army."

"*Ja*," said Hans. "Must go back. Must play *Trommel*."

"But his army is moving on!" said Josiah. "Even if he escapes, there will be nowhere for him to go."

"Turn him over to the Green Mountain Boys," growled Grandfather. "He's nothing but a mercenary anyway."

Hans flushed. Mercenary was one of the first English words he had learned from the British soldiers.

"Mr. Hawkins said Warner's headed for Manchester. Are we going to chase him all that way just to hand over a drummer boy?" said Mother. "I can't spare the time, and neither can Josiah. And what would Colonel Warner do with him anyway? Aren't musicians protected because they're unarmed?"

"I don't know," said Grandfather. "We never had any brass bands back when I was fighting the Indians. Good thing too," he snorted.

"Seth Warner and the others have more important things to worry about. I say we send Hans back to his own army as soon as he's well enough," said Mother.

"That's treason!" cried Grandfather. "What are you thinking of, woman?"

"I'm thinking of us," she snapped. "And this boy. He doesn't belong here. As you said, his duty is to escape, but if he escaped into these woods, it would be sure death for him. I would never do that even to my worst enemy. No, we must take him back to his own people."

Grandfather made no reply.

Mother turned to Josiah. "You know these woods better than anyone. Can you get Hans back to his camp without being seen?"

"Surely," replied Josiah eagerly.

"Then that's settled," said Mother. "Hans is doing very well. At this rate he should be able to travel soon. I'm sure the army won't leave immediately, but they won't wait too long. We'll have to get him back as soon as possible." She turned to Hans. "Josiah will take you to your army."

"*Ja,* army," said Hans. "Find army. Play *Trommel.*"

"What if his army has moved on?" asked Josiah.

"We'll worry about that when it happens," said Mother.

As evening approached, Josiah and Hans sat and carried on a halting conversation, using words and gestures to communicate. Hans told Josiah about the small village in Brunswick where he was raised. He described what an honor it was to be chosen as drummer boy for Baron von Riedesel. Josiah listened attentively as Hans told him of his military life. He spoke of learning some English from British soldiers and of the hardships of the past winter in Montreal.

"And then you came down here," said Josiah. "What was it like?"

Hans frowned. "Bad. Very hot. The soldiers have been mean. All scared—scream all the time, 'Faster, faster!' It is strange—sit all winter, do nothing, then bam"—he clapped his hands—"march, march, march."

"So how did you end up in the woods?" asked Josiah.

"I do not know." Hans shook his head. "I fall, lose *Trommel*. Do not know." He fell silent as he tried to remember.

"You are far from home. Don't you miss your family? Your mother?"

"*Ja*, miss mother. Miss food," replied Hans with a laugh. He made a face. "*Englisch*, cook bad. No bratwurst."

"Well, I don't have bratwurst either, Hans," said Mother. "We only have wild leek soup and hardtack."

Hans shrugged. "It is the soldier-life," he said matter-of-factly as Mother and Josiah laughed.

After supper Hans was recovered enough to take a short walk outside. Josiah showed him the havoc the raiders had left behind and described what the farm had looked like before.

Hans appeared unaffected by the destruction. "It is a good—what do you say? Tact. It is part of war," he stated.

Josiah gaped at him. "How can you say that? We worked so hard here, and the raiders had no reason to ruin it!"

"*Ja*," said Hans, "but, if orders, you do the same. I am sorry for you—farm hurt—but bugs, fire also hurt farms, no?" He smiled at Josiah. "Not me. It has not been my doing."

Josiah relented. "I know. It's hard to think of you as my enemy."

"No, not enemy. Other people enemies, not us," said Hans. He turned to the cornfield. "How can you plant a field?" he asked as they surveyed the trodden corn. "It is lot of work."

"It's not that bad," said Josiah. "The oxen really do the work. It's easier than marching twenty miles in the heat."

Hans laughed. "I take the marching."

Josiah looked at him in surprise. "Really?"

"*Ja*, I am not farmer," said Hans. "I am soldier."

Josiah looked out at the field and then down at his own callused hands. "I guess that's the difference between us. I'd like to be a soldier, but only if I can come back to the farm after the war is over. I suppose that does make me a farmer after all."

"You are farmer, I am soldier," said Hans, slapping Josiah on the back. "But still friends," he added as they returned to the cabin.

Night fell over the mountains once again. Thunder rumbled in the distance, as if it were echoing the battle that had taken place. Josiah and Hans slept while the last stages of the battle played themselves out. The Americans ran through the night while the British posted sentries and patrolled the ridge. And on the battlefield, those who could tended the wounded and buried the dead.

—CHAPTER 11—

The next morning Hans was well enough to travel. He and Josiah were ready to leave shortly after dawn. Hans looked pale in the dim light.

"Are you sure you can make it?" asked Josiah.

Hans nodded.

Mother handed Hans a small pouch. "This is for your head. When it hurts, chew a little of the bark."

She turned to Josiah. "Take him over the ridge, but stay out of sight. Make sure his army is still there, and then take him as far as the brook. He can follow it back to his camp. Then come straight home, you hear?"

"Yes'm," replied Josiah.

Mother walked the two boys out to the road and hugged them both. "Godspeed!" she cried, waving them on their way. "Remember, Josiah, hurry home!"

Josiah and Hans went up the path. This is certainly a lot easier than the last trip, thought Josiah.

They rested often. Even though Hans insisted "Head good," Josiah did not want to rush him.

As they rounded the north end of Pittsford Ridge, Josiah climbed a tree and looked out. The battlefield had turned into a huge camp with masses of men milling around. The dead were gone, and the wounded lay in rows.

"If Mr. Hawkins was right, those should all be British and German soldiers," said Josiah.

Josiah climbed down and the boys continued on, taking more care to be quiet. They paused on a small hill.

"Just a little way more," said Josiah. "The brook runs on the other side of that rise."

Hans put a hand on Josiah's arm.

"Wait," he said. He looked down at his bloodstained tunic and removed a small medal. He held it out to Josiah.

"Friend. You remember me."

Josiah took the medal. "Thank you," he said. "But I have nothing to give you."

Hans smiled. "You help me. You have taken me back to army. You have given me freedom."

Josiah grinned. "I guess that's a pretty good gift at that. Let's go."

They went a short distance to a small, swift stream.

"This is the source of the brook. It gets wider down there," said Josiah. "Just follow the water, and you'll run right into your camp."

The boys shook hands, and Hans turned to go.

"Halt!" A soldier suddenly stepped out of the trees in front of Hans, barring his way with a bayonet.

Josiah stepped back to flee, but strong arms grabbed him from behind.

"Well, well, what have we here?" the soldier with the bayonet said. "Looks like one of the Germans. And a rebel too! Now, what were you two doing here? Trying to desert?" The sentry sneered at Hans.

A blast of furious German exploded from Hans. His eyes flashed as he snapped at the soldier.

The sentry stepped back. "All right, all right. You can go, but you'll have some explaining to do, I don't doubt." He motioned to Hans to proceed and turned to Josiah.

"But you," he said nastily, "you are coming with us."

Josiah struggled, but his captor was too strong for him. He stomped and kicked at the man's feet and legs, but the burly soldier just laughed.

"It will take more than a little wisp of a boy to hurt old Jack" was all he said.

Hans looked back at Josiah in dismay, but there was nothing he could do to free him. He gave one last look and then turned up the path Josiah had shown him.

Jack and the other soldier each took one of Josiah's arms in an iron grip. Although he still struggled, they propelled him down the path. They broke out of the trees and dragged him none too gently up a slope to a cabin. It was the Sellecks' cabin, now headquarters for the enemy.

They brought Josiah before an officer who was standing outside the cabin. Jack saluted smartly.

"Enemy prisoner, sir. We found him in the woods."

The officer stared down at Josiah. "Name?" he said.

Jack elbowed Josiah in the ribs. "Better answer, boy."

"Josiah Freeman," replied Josiah. Jack punched him again and he added, "Sir."

"Where was he found?"

"Coming down off the ridge, sir," said Jack. "He was in the company of one of the Germans."

The officer raised his eyebrows. "Oh, really? Perhaps we have uncovered a spy ring then. This boy is old enough to be spying for the rebels." The officer sneered as he pronounced the last word. "Were you, boy?"

Josiah stood tall and stared defiantly at him. Let this Englishman wonder if any Americans remained in the woods.

"I see. And I take it you will not swear loyalty to your king, either."

This time Josiah replied firmly, "No, sir."

"Well, then, put him with the rest of the traitors. If he tries to run away, whip him and tie him to a tree." The officer dismissed them with a wave of his hand.

Josiah raged and struggled against his captors. How dare he treat him like a dog! Tied to a tree, indeed!

Jack laughed and held him firmly. "If you're smart, you'll behave yourself, sonny. There's no getting away, you know."

"I'll find a way!" declared Josiah hotly.

The two men laughed and pulled Josiah up to the crest of the hill. At the top they paused.

This side of the hill had been hidden from Josiah's sight earlier, and he recoiled at what he saw now. Here was the last remnant of the rearguard force. This was what was left of the brave American forces—over two hundred men herded together in a group, surrounded by armed guards.

Most of the prisoners lay wounded or sick. All of them were tattered and bedraggled, a beaten army. A few makeshift tents stood in the center, with rows of men fanned out all around. The guards tightly patrolled the edges of the camp.

Josiah was speechless with dismay. There would be no escape from here!

Jack chuckled. "Decided to be a good boy, eh?"

They led Josiah between rows of men. Josiah looked down at them, and his heart lurched. Some lay motionless, while others rolled in pain and reached out to them, begging for water. Josiah scanned the rows for his father but did not see him.

They reached the group of tents, and the two captors thrust Josiah forward, sending him sprawling on the ground. "Here's another for you," they called out and walked away.

Josiah looked up. Hands reached to help him to his feet.

"Don't worry son, we'll take care of you." A large bearded man in buckskins patted him on the shoulder. "Corporal, go tell the colonel we've got another prisoner."

"Yes, sir!" The corporal saluted and hobbled away, one bandaged leg dragging behind.

"Now, then." The bearded man turned back to Josiah and studied his face intently. "You look familiar. What's your name, boy?"

"Josiah Freeman, sir," Josiah replied.

"I knew it!" exclaimed the man. "Matthew's son!" He threw one arm around Josiah and hugged him tightly. Josiah's eyes grew wide.

"I'm William Johnson. Remember me? No, of course you don't. You were just a little fellow when I last saw you. Aye, but you've got the look of your father about you."

"Mr. Johnson! I've heard my father speak of you often. How do you do, sir?" Josiah held out his hand.

The bearded man laughed and shook Josiah's hand warmly. "By golly, you're all grown up! But it's Captain Johnson now. And what are you doing here in the middle of a war? Your father was hoping you all had gone to safety somewhere."

"It's a long story, sir. But what about Father? Is he here?"

"No, he isn't," replied the captain. "At least not among the wounded. I don't know what happened to him. I'm sorry, Josiah, but maybe there's someone here who knows for sure."

"Why are you here, sir?" asked Josiah.

"I was hit just as we were heading back toward the ridge." Captain Johnson motioned to his shoulder, and Josiah saw a bandage beneath the ragged sleeve. "It was

61

a clean wound, but it put me out of the action. But come along, you need to report to the colonel."

"Colonel Warner?" Josiah's eyes widened.

"No, he got away to Manchester. I'm speaking of Colonel Hale of the Second New Hampshire. He was in charge of the sick and the wounded, and the British tricked him into surrendering. He's the commanding officer here."

They approached the largest tent, and Captain Johnson saluted. A young man stepped forward. He wore the blue and white New Hampshire militia uniform.

"I'm Colonel Hale," he said kindly to Josiah. "It seems Colonel Warner is recruiting young boys now."

"No, sir." Josiah flushed. "I mean, I'm not a soldier. I wish I was, only, I mean . . ." He flushed deeper and stammered, "I—I'm Josiah Freeman. I live over the ridge."

"And curiosity brought you here?" asked the colonel.

"Not exactly, sir. I was looking for my father."

Captain Johnson interrupted, "His father is Captain Freeman of Seth Warner's regiment."

Colonel Hale nodded. "Did you find him?"

"No, sir, but as I was leaving I found Hans. He was wounded, sir."

"Hans? A German?"

"Yes, sir, a drummer boy. I couldn't leave him there. He would have died." As the story tumbled out, the group around Josiah grew.

"So you patched up your prisoner and then brought him back to his army," concluded the colonel.

"Yes, sir," said Josiah. Surrounded by these men who

had suffered so much at the hands of the Germans, helping Hans seemed traitorous now, not noble.

The colonel studied Josiah's face. "There is nothing wrong with helping a wounded man, enemy or not," he said. "It is an honorable thing to do. Since there was no one to turn him over to, as I see it, you had no choice but to bring him back. I imagine Captain Johnson will vouch for your loyalty." He sighed. "It's a pity that you got caught. The British have posted sentries all over the ridge. They expect a counterattack, I presume. I trust you did not inform them otherwise?"

"No, sir."

"I shall make an appeal to the British commander on your behalf," said the colonel. "Perhaps he will be reasonable and release you. In the meantime, I'll put you in the care of Captain Johnson. A strong young man with sound arms and legs is a great asset just now. I'm sure he can find a job for you helping the wounded." He waved his dismissal.

"Yes, sir!" said Josiah. He might not be able to fight with the army, but at least now he could help some men who really needed it.

— CHAPTER 12 —

Captain Johnson led Josiah to the edge of the camp. "Our water carriers will be returning here soon," he said. "We have a great need for water. This hot weather does us no good. Many of these men are not wounded. They are recovering from an attack of the measles that swept through Ticonderoga last month. Most of them are well enough to walk, but they haven't fully recovered yet. Some resumed their duties and tried to fight, but the disease weakened them, and it will take them longer to recover from their wounds. The British doctors have done what they can, but their soldiers have first priority."

"I did not think they would help you at all," said Josiah. "The British soldiers I saw were very mean."

"Oh, you mustn't think like that. They have treated us well, considering. They provide food and shelter for the very sick. But this is war, son. War is a mean business."

"I have certainly seen that," said Josiah.

"You must remember also that the British regard us as traitors to the king. They cannot understand why we fight against him."

"And traitors are worse than enemy soldiers of another land?"

"That's right." Captain Johnson sighed. "But we're out of the fighting for now. Some of us will be sent to England and tried in court for treason."

"Oh, no!" cried Josiah in dismay. "Is there any way to escape?"

"Of course we will try if we have the chance, but right now we are heavily guarded. I have men who need my help right now, so I cannot leave them. But once they are better, I will try to get all of us free. But if I don't succeed, I have one consoling thought."

"What's that?" asked Josiah.

"If the British are holding us captive, they must guard us. And then there are fewer guns for them to use in battle."

"Oh," said Josiah.

"We cannot always follow the path we want in life," said the captain. "I am resigned to my fate. You, on the other hand, have no reason to stay."

"And every reason to leave," added Josiah.

Captain Johnson nodded. "Right now we are surrounded. Those guns are loaded, and the soldiers will shoot you if you run. But if you ever have the chance to get away, take it and Godspeed."

"Thank you, sir," said Josiah. "Do you think they would follow me back to the farm?"

"They probably wouldn't follow you over the ridge. If you can make it to the top, you should be safe." Captain Johnson pointed. "I see the water carriers coming up now."

A group of five men carrying canvas buckets full of water walked up the rise. They were accompanied by two British soldiers with bayonets. They poured the water into an animal trough that had belonged to one of the neighboring farms. The captain directed Josiah to take the place of one of the men, and he joined the group.

One of the other carriers looked at Josiah intently. He fell into step with Josiah.

"I'm Sergeant John Miller. What is your name, boy?" he asked.

"Josiah Freeman, sir," he replied.

"Ah, that explains it. You look like your father. I'd know you for Matthew's son anywhere."

Josiah's heart swelled. "Do you know what happened to my father, sir?" he asked eagerly.

"I was right beside him all the way to the ridge," Miller replied. "Two British grenadiers were right behind us. The ridge was clouded in smoke, and it was hard to see. I tripped and fell. Your father came back to help me, but I told him to go on. I had wrenched my ankle, and I knew I would slow him down. No sense in us both being captured, I said, so he went on. As far as I know, he's on his way to the rendezvous right now."

"That's a relief," said Josiah.

"So how do you come to be here?"

Josiah recounted the tale of his capture.

66

"Well, you landed yourself in a spot, all right," said Sergeant Miller. "I've been looking for a chance to escape all morning, but these boys here know their business."

One of the guards turned and smiled. He had been listening to their conversation.

"That's right, matey. There's no escaping us, even if you shouldn't be here in the first place, which it's not for me to say," he said.

"You heard the boy's story, Corporal. Why don't you just turn your back for a moment?" said Sergeant Miller.

The British guard snorted. "You're daft. Do you know what they do to ones as let prisoners escape? I'd like to live to see England again, thank you kindly."

By this time they had reached the brook, and Josiah dipped out his two buckets. It seemed an eternity ago that he had done this same task for Mother.

Mother. What would she do when she realized he was not coming back? She couldn't manage everything without him. He must escape!

On their return trip Josiah was silent. He watched for an opportunity to escape, but Sergeant Miller was right. The two British guards let nothing get by them. Perhaps tonight, he thought.

He made several trips to the brook for water. Finally, when the sun was high in the sky, the guard announced, "This is it, men. We'll stop for a rest after this trip."

As they neared the trough, Josiah saw Captain Johnson. Another man met him and took his buckets.

"The colonel wishes to see you," said the captain.

"You've done well this morning, Josiah. I'm glad to see that Matthew's son has grown up to be such a fine young man."

Josiah flushed. "Thank you, sir."

They arrived at the colonel's tent, and the captain ushered him in.

Colonel Hale sat at a rough wooden table. He put down a pen as Josiah entered. He looked tired, fatigue and worry etching deep lines in his youthful face.

"I've bad news, Josiah. The British have rejected my appeal for your release. Instead, they have ordered me to turn you over to the German commander without delay." He stood up and clasped his hands behind his back and paced back and forth.

"But why the Germans, sir?" asked Josiah.

"It seems the Germans think they have prior claim on you. They say their drummer boy took you prisoner."

Josiah stared, openmouthed. What treachery was this?

"But I took him prisoner, sir. He knows that!"

"Nevertheless, they claim otherwise. I don't know why they want you, but you're the prisoner of the Germans now!"

— CHAPTER 13 —

Josiah took leave of Colonel Hale, and the captain followed him out of the tent. A German soldier stood ready to lead him away.

Josiah shook hands with Captain Johnson. "I'm glad we met, Josiah. If you manage to get away somehow, could you get word to my family?"

Josiah nodded solemnly. "Mother can write them a letter. Will you be all right?"

"I'll be fine. God go with you, Josiah," he called as the German led Josiah away.

Josiah followed the escort and thought about Hans. How dare he say he had captured him! He said he was his friend, and now this!

The soldier led him through the British camp. The supply wagons were beginning to arrive, and one by one small tents were being raised.

The German camp was to the north of the British. Their supply wagons had not been far behind when their army arrived the day before. Already an orderly tent city was spread out in neat rows. Even so, one group appeared to be preparing to leave, striking their tents and packing up. Where to next? wondered Josiah.

Josiah looked for Hans, but he was nowhere in sight. As he and the guard walked past the tents, Josiah heard only the strange words and unfamiliar sounds of the foreign army.

A large tent festooned with several bright flags stood in the center. A smartly uniformed guard stood at attention before it. Josiah's escort stopped.

They barked at each other while Josiah looked around. No escape from here, either. The camp was crowded with armed soldiers.

The sentry disappeared inside and returned after a moment.

"You, go in," he pointed to Josiah.

Josiah entered the tent and stepped onto a richly patterned carpet. He looked down in surprise. The whole tent was luxuriously furnished. A bed draped with rich coverings stood on one side, with a carved table next to it that held a delicate porcelain washbowl and pitcher.

The tent was dominated by an ornate desk, and from this rose a man.

"So you are Yosiah, *ja?*" The man came around the desk and held out his hand.

Confused, Josiah shook it. The man was of medium

height, but stocky. His elaborate uniform tunic was hung with several insignia and medals.

Josiah looked up into a beaming face. The cheeks were flushed with color, but the eyes were alert, taking in every detail as they raked over Josiah.

"I am Major General Friedrich Adolf von Riedesel. You may call me 'sir.'" He chuckled. "Now what do I do with you, eh?"

Josiah was speechless. This was the man whom Hans admired so much, undoubtedly the commander of the German army. He exuded strength and power, and he was a man who had no use for fools.

"First we eat." The baron motioned to the small table. There were two places set and a covered tray. A silent man-at-arms held out a chair for the baron and slipped quietly around to do the same for Josiah. He deftly uncovered the tray and held it out to the baron.

"It is not much. It is only beef joint and wild greens," said the Baron. "It is better than *Englisch. Englisch* cook bad." He parroted Hans's words of the day before.

The beef was done to a turn. The aroma engulfed Josiah. He had not had fresh beef in months. Where had the Germans gotten this meat? For all he knew, this was one of Father's oxen!

"Eat, eat," said the baron, plunging in.

"Now, Yosiah Freeman," he said after a few bites, "you want to be free man, *ja*?" The baron laughed at his joke.

Josiah grinned weakly. He nibbled at the wild greens, but the food stuck in his throat.

"You rebels fight very bravely. I am a military man, and I have fought many battles. Never I have seen such courage and honor. Your Colonel Francis was a brave man. He has stood in front of his men, taken bullets himself to protect his men." The baron shook his head. "A true warrior and a loss to the world. I have given him a military burial," added the baron. "Some *Englisch* do not like this. Some say he is a traitor, not a soldier. But he has been very brave."

Josiah pushed the greens around his plate with a hard biscuit.

The man-at-arms stepped forward to pour wine for the baron.

"So why have you rebelled against your king? Why all this fighting?"

Josiah swallowed. "We want to be free, sir."

"But it is your duty to obey your king!"

"King George has been very mean to us, sir. He only wants our money. He has put a tax on everything. And he sent soldiers to live in our homes. We feel like prisoners in our own land."

"But you are his colonies. He has a right to do what he wants," replied the baron.

"No he doesn't, sir," said Josiah.

"Ah, I have not understood you rebels. You cannot win this war. The king will send many more soldiers and guns. And then it will be worse for you."

"We will win this war!" replied Josiah.

The baron made no reply but studied Josiah intently.

"We will win because we are fighting for what we

believe in. We are not fighting for honor or glory. We are fighting for our homes."

"Ah, still I have not understood," said the baron, shaking his head. He leaned back in his chair and wiped his hands on a linen cloth.

"Now, what about you, Yosiah? You are a rebel spy and my prisoner. What shall I do with you? You know that the sentence for spying is death!"

Josiah gulped but remained silent.

"I could have shot you for spying," said the baron, rising and going to his desk. "If I send you back to the *Englisch*, they will put you on a prison ship. Maybe even send you to England."

The man-at-arms stepped forward to clear the table, and Josiah rose. He stood before the baron, fists clenched.

"But that is waste," said the baron, picking up his pen. "Hans has told me what a bright boy you are. He has told me many things."

Color slowly mounted in Josiah's cheeks. The baron noted his anger with satisfaction.

"*Ja*, Hans has told me about your mother and grandfather and your farm. I know where it is."

Josiah bristled. "We helped Hans! He would have died wandering around in the woods if I hadn't found him. My mother nursed him back to health! He had no right to tell you where we live. Besides"—Josiah's eyes narrowed—"he was *my* prisoner."

"No, no, no, you have not understood." The baron's eyes grew cold. "Some might think that Hans has deserted the army, gone away. But this has not happened.

Hans has gone to capture a rebel spy and has brought him back. It is here in the report." He patted a bound book on his desk. "Very clever, no?"

Josiah stared at the baron. So he was being used! Someone had suspected Hans of running away, not just wandering off in a daze. But the commander could not let such a charge be brought against his handpicked recruit. So instead of Hans deserting and being captured, he had rooted out a dangerous enemy spy!

Josiah bit his lip. If he insisted on the truth, what would happen to Hans? A trial, surely—maybe even a death sentence. The conflicting emotions crossed his face.

"I know you will cooperate with me." The baron folded his hands and leaned forward. "I need a bright boy to tell me how the rebels think. It is very important to know how the enemy thinks."

Josiah let out his breath slowly. Work with the baron against his people? No, let Hans claim him as a prisoner if he liked, but he would not betray his own people.

"Never!" he spat out.

The baron raised his eyebrows. "Oh? We shall see about that. Corporal," he barked.

The sentry appeared in the doorway, and the baron spoke to him quickly. He rose and came around his desk. "The corporal will take you to your new quarters. Of course he will remain with you to make sure you are comfortable."

"You mean to guard me," said Josiah.

"Ah, well, if you insist. But one day you will no longer

need a guard, you know." The baron put out his hand. "It was a pleasure to meet you, Yosiah."

Josiah stared at the extended hand.

"Come, now, we are all honorable gentlemen, Yosiah. This is war, we cannot always have everything we want. Let us part for now as friends," said the baron, taking Josiah's reluctant hand in his.

"Yes, sir," said Josiah grudgingly. Then he turned and followed the guard out the door as the baron softly laughed behind him.

——CHAPTER 14——

The guard led Josiah to a small tent that stood away from the main camp. He motioned for Josiah to enter.

There were no fancy beds in this tent. This was the tent of a common foot soldier. About six feet wide and nine feet long, it normally housed six men. There was only one entrance, and the tent held only a blanket neatly folded in one corner.

Josiah dropped to the ground as the guard took up his post outside. He put his arms on his knees and cradled his head. Now what?

So much had happened to him. Images of the last three days whirled in his head. His peaceful life on the farm seemed like a distant memory. After imagining the glories of war, he had found nothing in it but destruction, blood, and betrayal.

Oh well, he thought. I can't dwell on it right now. I must escape from here! But how?

If only I had a knife, he thought. I could be out of this tent and into the trees before the guard could turn around. But his pockets were empty. Even Hans's medal had been taken from him.

Josiah crawled over and peeped through the tent flaps. If he could distract the guard, he could run for it. He might get far enough away before they shot at him. Overpowering the guard was out of the question, even if he hadn't been armed.

As Josiah mulled over his problem, someone approached the tent. He heard Hans's voice address the guard. Hans! What was he doing here?

The guard replied and, to Josiah's surprise, walked away. Hans lifted the flap of the tent and stepped in, a big smile on his face.

"Hallo, Yosiah," he said.

"You lousy rat!" roared Josiah. He jumped up and flew at Hans, knocking him to the ground. They rolled on the floor of the small tent.

"Wait! No hurt!" cried Hans. "Let me talk."

Josiah pinned him to the ground by the shoulders.

"I help you," gasped Hans. "I get you from *Englisch*."

"What's all this about me being your prisoner? And what about making me work for the baron? He threatened my family!"

"*Nein, nein,* his idea. I have said I am caught, but he said no. Bad for soldier, leave army. He help me."

"But what does that have to do with me?"

"I get you from *Englisch*. *Englisch* have many guards. No escape. So baron say you my prisoner."

"But what about all that stuff he said about me being a spy and helping him?"

"He make sure I told the truth. You can be soldier now, with me," said Hans.

Josiah released Hans's shoulders and sat back on his heels. He shook his head. "Except you're not exactly on the right side. No, thank you. You tell the baron he can keep his dirty job."

Hans sat up. "You escape then."

"What about the guard?"

"I have sent him away. Back soon. Here." Hans dug into his pocket and held out his hand. "This is two times I give to you."

It was Hans's medal. Josiah took it, smiling.

"Thank you. But won't you get in trouble for letting me escape?"

"I have not let you. You are a big rebel." Hans punched the air. "You have knocked poor Hans over, *ja?*" He pushed Josiah toward the tent flap. "Go now."

"Good-bye, Hans." Josiah stuck out his hand.

Hans shook it. "Good-bye, Yosiah. Now hurry!"

Josiah crouched low and looked outside the tent. The whole camp was busy with their own concerns, and the little tent stood far enough away that no one noticed Josiah scurry into the nearby bushes.

Josiah paused behind a bush to look back. He had been just in time. The guard was coming back, and he broke into a trot as he neared the unguarded tent.

Josiah stayed long enough to hear Hans cry out in mock pain, then he ran further into the woods, dashing from tree to tree. Breathless, he scrambled behind a large rock and peered out.

He heard faraway shouts as the guard gave the alarm in the camp, and he jumped as an answering cry in English came from the woods just behind him. It was a British patrol! Josiah shrank back as he realized how close he had come to running right into them.

He crouched farther down as the patrol crashed through the woods. They stopped just yards away from his rock, and Josiah held his breath.

"Which way did he go? Where is he?" came the voices.

Josiah heard an excited German reply, then Hans's voice said clearly, "There! I see him! After me!"

Josiah closed his eyes. This is it, he thought. They've got me now. He crouched, every fiber tense.

Time stood still as he waited for a hand to drag him from his hiding place, but no one came near. Instead, it sounded as if the patrol were going farther away. They were! Hans was leading them away!

Josiah opened his eyes and took a deep breath. So Hans had not betrayed him after all. He peered over the edge of the rock. The woods were silent, only a cloud of midges dancing in the filtered sunlight. He cautiously crept out of his hiding place. The patrol would soon be back, and he had to use the head start that Hans had given him. He breathed a silent thank you to his friend, then hurried up Pittsford Ridge.

—CHAPTER 15—

Hans led the patrol through the wood. From time to time he stopped and pointed. "What is that?" he would say and dart off in a new direction. But he knew that he couldn't lead them on the chase for long. Finally, when he thought he'd given Josiah enough time to escape, he stopped and threw up his arms.

"He has escaped. No trail anymore."

The British soldiers grumbled, but Hans smiled and shook his head. "These Americans," he said, "like foxes."

He soothed them by offering them his beer ration. The soldiers agreed readily, and no more mention was made of the wild-goose chase. When Hans offered them his next day's rations as well, it was enough to make them forget that they had been chasing an escaped prisoner at all.

When they returned to the camp, Hans directed the British soldiers to his friend the quartermaster, then went with the German corporal to the baron.

They found him directing the removal of his tent. Hans and the corporal saluted.

"I regret to inform you that the enemy spy has escaped, sir," Hans stated in formal German.

The baron raised one eyebrow and looked at Hans. "Escaped, has he? Ah, well, that is a pity."

"The drummer boy knows where he lives," said the corporal eagerly. "Shall we pursue him?"

The baron frowned and looked toward the tent, where two soldiers were carrying away his desk. "No, corporal, he is probably quite far away by now. It would be a waste of time, and I am quite anxious to get moving." He smiled. "You will be rewarded for your efforts, corporal. That is all." The corporal nodded, half shrugging, saluted smartly, and left.

The baron turned to Hans. "So, your prisoner escaped?"

"He hit me on the head, sir," replied Hans.

"Ah, well, these things happen," replied the baron. "But because you let yourself be hit, you will be responsible for striking that tent. Then return to your unit. We are leaving immediately. The sooner we are out of this wilderness, the better."

Hans saluted. The baron returned his salute. Then, after looking to make sure no one was watching, he winked and grinned.

Hans returned his grin, then ran off to get ready to march again.

The baron looked up at the ridge, bright in the afternoon sun. "Godspeed, Yosiah," he murmured softly. "And good luck, my little rebel." Then, with a chuckle, he turned back to his tent.

— Chapter 16 —

Josiah moved cautiously up the ridge. In some spots he had to almost crawl from ledge to ledge. He had not seen or heard any more British patrols.

It was late afternoon before he reached the top. He could not resist the temptation to look back, so he climbed a tall tree.

The sun hung in the western sky. Clouds were moving in, promising rain. Down below, the huge camp was in motion. Tents were going up and coming down. Detachments of men moved in and out. Officers barked orders, soldiers hurried to obey.

Josiah looked toward the American section. He made out the center tent where Colonel Hale was. There were more tents encircling it now. At least some of the wounded would be protected from the rain.

Tomorrow the armies would move on. The coming rain would wash the blood from the ground, and soon there would be no sign that a battle had taken place, or that men had died here.

Josiah thought of Captain Johnson. Tomorrow he would march under guard with his men. Although they were marching in captivity, Josiah knew the captain would not be defeated. Somehow, somewhere, he would be free again, perhaps soon enough to rejoin Josiah's father and the others with Seth Warner.

And Hans. Josiah smiled at the thought of his friend running headlong through the woods with the patrol right behind him. He would fall back into the pattern of military life and go on from one camp to another. Will he remember me? wondered Josiah.

Josiah breathed a prayer for his friends. "Keep them safe, O Lord," he whispered. "And make a short end to this war."

Josiah looked at the green mountains. What was his future? Where was he going?

Home, his heart immediately answered. Home to Mother and Grandfather and the farm. He sighed when he thought of the hard work ahead to rebuild their farm, but the thought of his own horse heartened him. Even Father would now have to admit that he could handle the responsibility.

Josiah climbed down the tree and turned toward home. What a tale he would have for Grandfather! Mother would scold him for letting himself be captured, but at least Grandfather would listen eagerly.

And then in years to come, they would tell the story of the Battle of Hubbardton. The tale would grow with the telling, until all other adventures paled in comparison.

But now Josiah knew that the story of the most important battle would not be retold. The real battle of his life lay just below him—the battle to keep the farm going. No one would remember his struggles against nature and adversity, but without him and thousands of others like him, the battles of the War for Independence would be meaningless. Without the determination to build new homes and forge a strong new nation, this war would be fought in vain.

The first drops of rain pattered on the leaves around Josiah. He lifted his face to the cooling breeze and breathed deeply. Refreshed, he bounded down the ridge toward his waiting home—and a battle worth fighting.

— *E*PILOGUE —

"Andrea! You're daydreaming again!" Julie pulled her friend away from the diorama. "Come look at this neat map."

Julie dragged Andrea to a large relief map. She pushed a button, and a recording told the story of the Battle of Hubbardton, Vermont. It told about the American rear guard retreating from Fort Ticonderoga and their British and German pursuers. Lights flashed to show the movement of the battle across the terrain.

Andrea was fascinated by the chasing lights. She pushed the button to see it again, but Julie grabbed her arm.

"Come on. Everyone's going outside."

I wonder where old great-great-what's-his-name fought in the battle? thought Andrea as Julie led her out.

Julie ran up the hill, and Andrea followed slowly. At the top of the hill ran a long stone wall.

This must be the stone wall they fought behind. She sat down on a nearby bench and looked out at the distant mountains. What had this looked like with all the soldiers? She turned around on the bench. That's Pittsford Ridge, she thought. Looks pretty steep.

Heather and Julie ran up to her. "There you are!" they exclaimed.

"It's almost time to go. Did you hear about Billy?" asked Julie.

Heather added, "He ate some berries that weren't ripe and got sick in the bushes."

"Boy, was Miss Cline mad," said Julie. "She made him go sit on the bus."

"She called him a goat, you know, Billy goat?" said Heather.

"More like Billy the Kid," said Andrea.

The girls giggled and headed down the hill to the bus.

Andrea looked back. What would the people who fought here think if they could see us here? she wondered. She stopped and listened, but the guns of that July day were long silent. All she heard was the laughter of her friends.

I guess that's why they fought and died, she thought. So we could be happy and free.

Andrea boarded the bus with the rest of the children. As they drove away, leaving the rolling hills behind, peace fell on the meadow once more.

── AFTERWORD ──

As a rearguard action, the Battle of Hubbardton is now considered a success for the Americans. It delayed the British and German troops long enough to allow the main body of the American army to retreat from Fort Ticonderoga and regroup farther south. This American army then defeated the British later that summer at the Battle of Bennington. In October 1777, the British under General John Burgoyne surrendered at Saratoga, New York.

Colonel Nathan Hale of New Hampshire, who was in charge of the sick and wounded during the retreat from Fort Ticonderoga, was captured during the Battle of Hubbardton. He died in prison in September 1780.

After Burgoyne surrendered at Saratoga, his eight thousand troops were marched to Virginia. These included the German troops under his command. These men were not well guarded along the way, and many may have simply slipped away. Indeed, many Americans today can trace their family history back to the German soldiers who chose to stay in the New World.

The Hubbardton Battlefield Monument is open to the public from mid-May through mid-October. It is located in East Hubbardton, Vermont, north of Route 4 in Castleton. For more information write:

Vermont Division for Historic Preservation
Montpelier, Vermont 05609-1201